Return of the Yin

Return of the Yin

A Tale of
Peace and Hope
for a Troubled World

Diane Wolverton

The M.O.T.H.E.R.
Publishing Co., Inc.
Rock Springs, Wyoming

Published 2003 by The M.O.T.H.E.R. Publishing Co.,
Inc.

Inquires should be addressed to
The M.O.T.H.E.R. Publishing Co., Inc.
P.O. Box 477, Rock Springs, Wyoming 82902-0477
www.motherpublishing.com

First paperback edition 2003
ISBN: 0-9718431-4-7
Library of Congress Control Number: 2003096582

1. Feminine Spirituality 2. Fiction/Fantasy
3. Visionary Fantasy 4. Mythology I. Title

Printed in the United States of America

To Bob
who has loved me
throughout my journey
and to women everywhere
who long for a world
of balance and peace.

Acknowledgements

Many wonderful people have helped me through the process of conceiving, writing, rewriting and publishing this book. I am humbled to be the recipient of such an outpouring of support and I am enormously grateful for the part everyone has played in the publication.

To Kayne Pyatt for being the first to read the manuscript and for greeting it with such enthusiasm. Her early encouragement gave me the confidence to go forward and her passion for supporting women authors is now providing the publishing vehicle to make this edition possible.

To Rosemary Bratton for her friendship, encouragement and loving investment in the publication.

To Judith Duerk for introducing me to the concept of the yin.

To the circle of women who acted as midwives on a mountain in Casper, Wyoming, helping me to give birth to the vision these pages contain: Ellen Besso, Darlene Determan, Judith Duerk, Diane Friedman, Arlene-Nicki Hagoski, Martha Illige-Saucier, Peggy McCarthy, Catherine Murray, Joy Price, Linda Simons, Elaine Stafford, Anne Stewartson and Robbie Ross Tisch.

To my mother, Emily Dial, my sisters Linda Byers and Suzanne Iovino and my mother-in-law, Marian Sheffield for their ongoing support, love and encouragement.

To my husband, Bob, for his steadfast belief in me and his editing help throughout the process.

And to the many women who have read the book, resonated with its message and who continue to share it with others in hope that the vision will someday become a reality.

Introduction

This story began to unfold in my mind shortly after Princess Diana's tragic death in 1997. Since then it has ripened, matured and become more relevant to our world. It came to me as a fairy tale, a format that seemed appropriate for the myth-like qualities of the themes involved. The tale contains strong allusions to the Princess, her life and her death; but it is not a story about her. Rather, it is about the archetypal feminine she represented, the yin energy she personified and the conflicted state she found herself in as she tried to find joy in a world dominated by values not her own.

Women today know well her experience. In different ways we each have felt the isolation, the sense of not belonging, the brutality and the fear. Like Diana, we long for balance and peace—and find them continually out of our grasp.

In my own journey, I have sought to find balance in an unbalanced world. I have struggled to gather up and hold on to my authentic self in spite of all the centrifugal forces pulling at me from different directions. In her beautiful book, *Gift from the Sea*, Ann Morrow Lindberg gives this condition a name. She calls it "torn-to-pieces-hood"—from the German word *Zerrissenheit*. Now, nearly fifty years after Lindberg's lament, this condition has not improved. In fact, in many ways, *Zerrissenheit* has only worsened.

In just the past few years we have experienced scandal in the White House, a contested presidential election, 9-11, war with Afghanistan and Iraq, war against terrorism, Enron, church scandals, environmental catastrophes and escalation of domestic violence, rape and violence of all kinds—all testaments to the gross imbalance in the world today.

There is hope. There is a vision for a balanced world contained in the pages of this small volume—a vision that is played out in the lives of the characters. The story gives the vision shape, makes it real and tells us, yes! Yes, it is possible for the women of the world to unite and galvanize for the purpose of restoring balance to the world.

It is possible to start a revolution. Simply. Quietly. Powerfully. It is possible to start a revolution in the spirit of the yin. No need to yell and scream or rail against anyone or anything. Just peacefully paying attention and shifting, shifting, shifting our resources. It is possible to start a revolution now. It is up to us.

Yes. Let us begin.

Chapter 1

Once upon a time there was a beautiful Princess who married a powerful Prince. The people of her kingdom watched her walk down the aisle. They said, "Now she will live happily ever after!"

She wore a crown of jewels and her dress had a very long train. Her hair was shimmering gold and her eyes were as clear and as blue as a sun-stained piece of glass. After the sacred wedding vows had been exchanged the Princess rode off with her new husband in a royal carriage. She was happy and her subjects were happy, too.

1

They knew that all good fairy tales end with the handsome prince scooping up his beautiful Princess and taking her off to the royal palace. The kingdom was filled with hope that the magic of happily-ever-after would envelop their land and everyone would share in tranquility and prosperity.

After the honeymoon the Princess settled into the palace. As she worked to set up her new home she realized she had never read a fairy tale that went beyond happily-ever-after. She had no clear instructions of what to do. She asked her husband, "What's next?"

The Prince replied, "You will bear me a son. There must be an heir to the throne."

"Of course!" said the Princess. Soon she gave birth to a prince—Nathaniel Paul—a boy destined to become the ruler of her kingdom.

The Princess loved being a mother. She devoted her energies and her spirit to raising her son to be happy and balanced and suited for a life of service to the kingdom. It appeared to all the world that her life was fulfilled. The people would have been surprised to learn that secretly the Princess began to feel lonely. She noticed that her Prince was drifting away. "What is it, my husband?" she asked. "Do I not please you?"

The Prince replied, "Don't bother me! Isn't it enough that I made you a Princess and the wealthiest woman in the kingdom? Just enjoy your jewels and leave me alone!"

The spurned Princess was hurt, but not discouraged. "I must learn how to please my Prince," she said. "I must learn how to be a good Princess. Then he will love me!" The first step, she decided, was to discover what a good Princess is. She set out to uncover the secret.

As the Princess began her quest, she came across a pack of wicked hyenas that roamed the kingdom. They were ugly and smelled of rotten flesh. They circled around the palace and waited for the Princess to emerge. They sniffed at all the doors and paced and panted in wait. Whenever she came out they followed her and chased her and frightened her.

They eyed her closely as she began her

search for what it meant to be a good Princess. Her first discovery was that a Princess must be beautiful. She set out to be the most beautiful Princess in the world. She searched far and wide for designers to prepare the most elegant clothes for her to wear. She found breathtaking gowns and exotic fabrics. She dazzled the kingdom with her beauty.

The hyenas sniffed and snorted and made clicking noises with their teeth. Then they burst into a frenzy of laughter, "You are beautiful indeed, but only because you spend, spend, spend on beautiful clothes. Haw! Haw! Haw!" They danced about and laughed. "And you are slender like a gazelle now, but you wait! You will become fat and wrinkled and even your lavish clothes won't help you then."

But in spite of all the cackling and spitting and clicking, the hyenas could not diminish the fact that the Princess truly was beautiful. The people of her kingdom noticed. And they were pleased.

One member of the kingdom who didn't notice, however, was the Prince. The

Princess was disappointed, but she vowed to continue her search for the secret of becoming a good Princess. "A good Princess must have compassion," she thought. She looked inside herself and found that she was full of compassion. She demonstrated it to her kingdom through tireless work to help people. She touched the sick and the rejected. She resonated with their pain. She brought light into their lives.

The hyenas mocked. Click, click, click went their teeth. "Haw, Haw, Haw" went their laughter. "She's a phony," they said. "She's just doing it to get attention. Haw! Haw! Haw!"

But even for all the laughing and mocking, the hyenas could not deny the fact that the Princess truly was helping people. The people of her kingdom noticed. And they were pleased.

One member of the kingdom who didn't notice, however, was the Prince. The Princess began to work even harder to learn the secret of becoming a good Princess and pleasing her Prince. But every move she made was mocked by the hyenas.

The constant taunting kept the Princess off balance. She began to feel trapped and helpless. Her life was not happily-ever-after at all. It was misery. She sobbed out a lonely cry for help.

Her cry reverberated among the heavens and was heard by Artemis, the Goddess of the Hunt. Artemis had not been on Earth in a very, very long time. In ages passed she had lived in the Kingdom and was revered and adored. Temples had been erected in her honor. It was her job as Goddess of the Hunt to make sure all hunts—whether conducted by humans or animals—were executed fairly and that no prey was ever taken out of harmony with the universal laws of fairness. In answer to the Princess' prayer, Artemis began to watch upon her from the heavens. She saw that the hyenas were not treating her fairly. They were stalking her and taunting her and taking pleasure in harming her.

The Goddess Artemis summoned the hyenas to her throne. She was a beautiful regal figure with long flowing black hair, eyes as black as pure obsidian, and luminous skin the color of bronze. "Why have you tormented the Princess," she demanded.

"Haw! Haw! Haw!" they mocked. "She's fair game. It goes with the territory. You cannot be a Princess without being hunted!"

"But, you are cheating!" said Artemis. "You are malicious and conniving. You are rewarded for undoing her!"

"Haw! Haw! Haw! She's fair game!" they chanted. "She is a woman!"

Artemis recoiled in shock. "How dare you speak such words! They are lies!"

The hyenas danced and laughed. "No! Not lies! Our words are true! The people in the Princess' kingdom are under a spell, and even though you are a Goddess, you cannot help her. You are bound by the spell of the land. You cannot keep us from her! Haw! Haw! Haw!"

Artemis could stand their laughing and mocking no longer. She sent them away. She knew that if there really was a spell cast upon the kingdom, she would be bound by it. It was universal law. She had just one power that was stronger than any spell. That was her divine power of protection

7

from death. She couldn't stop the hyenas from hounding the Princess, or tormenting her, or hurting her, but she could protect the Princess from death at the hands of her tormentors. She called upon this power and surrounded the Princess with an invisible cocoon of protection. She vowed to find the source of the spell in the kingdom. She vowed to put an end to it.

Chapter 2

Artemis decided first to seek the council of Mother Earth. She hoped that the mother of all creation would know what to do about the spell and that she might be able to offer an antidote—perhaps herbs or animal magic. Artemis entered the Mother's garden and was surprised at how unkempt it was. There were no beautiful smells of flowers and trees, but rather a scent of rot and decay. The bubbling brook that Artemis had remembered from eons past no longer bubbled—it foamed with a white froth. Diseased trees had replaced the lush groves Artemis remembered. The beautiful symphony of singing birds had been reduced to a single plaintive chirp coming from the bushes nearby.

She found Mother Earth curled up in a bed of grass asleep. Her long hair was white, her skin a pale gray.

"Mother Earth," Artemis whispered. "It's Artemis. I've come to visit you and seek your counsel."

Weakly, Mother Earth opened her eyes and turned to Artemis, "My dear, I have no wise counsel left. I am poisoned and I am dying. Slowly. Slowly. I am dying."

"What's poisoning you?" Artemis asked. "What is the antidote?"

"The antidote is in the breaking of the spell."

"What is the spell? How do I break it?" Artemis asked.

Mother Earth sighed a long, deep sigh. "I don't know. But I hope you can find it before it's too late for me. I don't have the strength to fight anymore.

"When I was a young mother the people of the kingdom came to me with reverence and awe. They celebrated my ability to bring forth creation, to bring forth food, to bring forth water. They lovingly sifted my soil through their fingers and raised up their hands to thank the heavens for the wondrous powers of Earth. They built temples to me. They honored me with holy days.

"Then things changed. They began to think they did not need to honor me any more. They felt they could take all they wanted, knowing I would produce more and more and more. That's my nature. To be abundant and alive. But they kept taking without gratitude and without honor. They didn't respect the balance—the gentle, tender balance of my systems. They were wasteful with my abundance. There was no reverence for what the Earth has given. All was taken for granted."

Artemis asked, "But haven't the people of the kingdom done anything to protect you. Aren't there laws?"

Mother Earth replied, "You cannot make laws to force people to care. The spell makes everyone think it's acceptable not to care. But it's not acceptable. It is deadly." Mother Earth laid her head wearily on the grass and closed her eyes.

Artemis stroked her head gently and whispered, "Rest now. Find comfort in your sleep. I promise I'll find what's behind the spell."

Chapter 3

Artemis left Mother Earth's garden and traveled to the home of her friend Athena, the Goddess of Wisdom. Athena was a very old and wise deity. Her long silver-white hair was swept up into a soft twist and fastened with a single stick. She wore a flowing violet dress with a wide sash at the waist. Athena was the deity responsible to oversee all the sources of knowledge and wisdom on Earth—the schools, the libraries, the universities, the books, the music, the museums, the mentors. She lived in the heavens above

Mount Olympus. Her study had a magical glass floor that gave her the power to view the kingdom below and to look into the houses of learning on Earth. Athena's assistant led Artemis into the study. There Artemis noticed rows and rows of books along the walls and a solitary desk in the center of the glass floor. Athena sat working at the desk. Artemis hesitated to step on the glass to approach Athena.

"Don't worry," said Athena, as she stood up. "It's strong enough to hold us both—and a hundred more!"

Artemis walked carefully over to the desk and greeted Athena with a hug. "Thank you for seeing me today. I have a lot on my mind and I need your help. Can you see the kingdom of the Princess up here? Do you know about the spell?"

Athena sighed. "Yes, Artemis, I know well the spell you speak of. But I have been powerless to break it."

Artemis persisted. "Can't you move within the institutions you oversee? Can't you bring them knowledge that would break the spell? Can't you teach the people

14

the secrets they need to know in order to free themselves from the spell's power?"

Athena turned toward her desk and said, "Let me show you something." She placed her hand on the cover of a great book. Slowly she flipped through the pages and Artemis could see that the pages contained photographs depicting scenes of people—people working together in the fields, building homes, teaching children and participating in rituals. The scenes represented a broad spectrum of peoples, places and eras in history. Artemis searched the scenes trying to take in the meaning when Athena stopped turning the pages and said, "Look closely at this one."

Artemis fixed her gaze on the photograph. She saw a panoramic view of a village. In the center of the village was a round court with a bustling marketplace. Merchants with display stands of wares made up the circumference of the circle. Children played in the center. The mothers were tending to their merchandise. One woman displayed shoes she had made, each carefully sewn and elegantly adorned with beads. Another woman displayed beautiful fabrics she had woven. Many women had clothing and food for sale.

Artemis was fascinated by the details in the photograph. She looked closer and closer. She could even make out the jewelry worn by one of the women in the picture. Artemis admired the many rings the woman wore—rings she could see clearly because the photograph had captured the woman's hand outstretched just as it was reaching toward a crying child as if to embrace him. Artemis started as she saw the hand suddenly move and complete the embrace. Next the scene took on sound. Artemis could hear the child's cries and the words of the mother comforting him.

"What's going on?" Artemis asked Athena. She was puzzled by the picture's ability to come to life.

"Just pay close attention," Athena replied. "You're watching history unfold."

"Whose history? Where? When?"

"It is the history of Earth," explained Athena. "When civilization was very, very young. It was before the spell was cast. Can you see the difference?"

Artemis looked closely as the scene played out before her. The marketplace was a center of noise and activity. Children ran to and fro, shoppers milled about and merchandise was everywhere. The exhibitors played several roles. Sometimes they visited with customers. Sometimes no customers were around so they sewed or prepared food or talked with one another. All kept watchful eyes on the children. If one child fell and scraped his knee, he knew he could run for comfort to the arms of any of the women there.

Outside of the marketplace Artemis saw several other activities under way. A group of men worked together to build a house. A midwife delivered a child and anointed it with herbs and loving energy. Two families joined together to collect berries. A group of women sat in a circle in silence, seeking wisdom and guidance from the heavens. They sang songs to the Goddess.

Off in the distance a band of foreigners approached the village. Artemis could tell they were different from the villagers by the way they dressed and the color of their skin. She wondered what mission they had in approaching the village.

Athena interrupted Artemis' thoughts. "Do you see anything in this scene that gives you a clue about the spell," Athena asked.

Artemis considered the question and replied, "I see cooperation. No one seems to be trying to take advantage of anyone else. The marketplace wares are out in the open, yet no one tries to steal them. The children play and all women watch them. I don't see anyone who seems to be exerting power or dominance. There is harmony; people are working together. It feels balanced."

"But what about the visitors coming from the north?" Athena said pointing to the top of the picture. "Do you think their arrival portends trouble? Look how different they are. Do you think the villagers will accept them?"

Artemis watched as the group progressed along the road and up a great hill. As they crested the hill, they stopped and surveyed the goings on in the village below.

Suddenly one of the members of the group let out a loud cry and motioned to the others to come along. They all started to whoop and holler and run down the hill toward the village. "Here it is," thought Artemis. "The attack!"

The startled villagers looked up and saw the intruders fast approaching them. Chaos erupted. Artemis expected them to run for cover or pick up their weapons to defend themselves. Instead she saw the villagers run toward the intruders. "Without weapons!" she gasped. "They will be slaughtered." It took all of her courage to keep her eyes focused on the scene. She did not want to see the blood flow. The two parties met at the edge of the village. More chaos erupted as they started to embrace one another and dance and sing with delight.

Artemis stared, her mouth agape in disbelief. The war she had anticipated turned out to be the most radiant outpouring of love she had ever seen. "How can this be?" she asked Athena. "Can it be true that people lived in peace? I thought this world's history was filled with war and conquering and pillaging and slavery. This doesn't fit."

"But it does fit," sighed Athena. "This is the way it once was. Look closely, you won't see a single weapon here. War and violence were unknown to these people. They held love as their highest value."

"What happened?" asked Artemis. "What caused humanity to abandon their value of love?"

"The spell," said Athena gravely.

"Where did the spell come from?" asked Artemis.

"The author of the spell is Ares, God of War," replied Athena. She pulled another book from her shelf and laid it on the desk. The book contained portraits of individuals—deities and leaders, mortals and immortals in history. Athena turned several pages and stopped at a portrait of a male deity. He looked confident and powerful. His dark hair framed his face with wild, defiant curls. Artemis thought she detected a slight glint of something sinister in his eyes.

Underneath the photograph was the caption: Ares, God of Conflict. Artemis pointed to the caption and said, "I thought you said he was the God of War."

"Ah, I did," said Athena. "But it didn't start that way. When Ares was born son of Zeus, his original assignment was to oversee discussion and conflict to make sure all participants were heard and fairness prevailed. But he had a different vision. His thirst for blood made him long for conflict to escalate into war. He thought if he could become the God of War, he would be the most powerful and most feared God in the universe. He hated peace and despised the fact that the world embraced love as its highest value. He knew that as long as love was the highest value, there would never be war. War cannot exist in an environment of love. Ares sought a method to remove love from its exalted position. He experimented with trying to elevate hate, envy, jealousy and greed into places of honor. But the contrast to love was too great and the people immediately rejected the change. They were too firmly grounded in their value system of love."

"How did he change that?" asked Artemis.

"One day Ares discovered a secret that

enabled him to change the course of history," Athena replied. "He discovered the secret of balance and how balance is essential to the well-being of this planet. He began to notice how balance is everywhere. The Earth's ecosystem depends on a myriad of delicate balances—chemical balances, temperature balances, atmospheric balances, and balances of light and dark. Then he saw how Earth's spiritual ecosystem depends on balance, too. It depends on the balance of the great forces of the yin and the yang. When in balance, these forces create spiritual wholeness all over the world. But when out of balance, spiritual chaos results. Ares surmised that if he could disturb the cosmic balance, the perfect value system of the people would be upset. War would become acceptable to a people who no longer valued love above all things.

"With a flourish Ares cast a spell that disturbed the perfect balance of the universe. He called for just a granule more of yang to be added to the balance. That tiny change has grown over the centuries into the huge cataclysmic imbalance we have today. Yang has a natural tendency to dominate and control the yin and when it was given that slight advantage, it began to run rampant. All the yang values of conquering, domination, perfectionism, progress, dominion, hierarchical structures, laws and rules, rationalness and linear thinking were elevated to positions of awe and respect. The yin values of cooperativeness, the ability to accept imperfection, the willingness to yield, a sense of *being* rather than *doing*—have been debased. That is why the hyenas have free reign with the Princess. They represent the yang values and she is the yin."

"Can't we get the balance back?" asked Artemis. "Can't we add more yin back into the equation."

"I have tried," said Athena. "It is just consumed by the yang, making the yang ever stronger. I do not know how to regain the balance. Ares is the only one who may know of a way to undo the spell."

"Then I will go to him!" exclaimed Artemis. "I will demand that he help me."

"Be careful, Artemis," cautioned Athena. "Don't build up your hopes too

23

high. The spell gains power every year—and it has been in force for millennia. Ares is unpredictable and dangerous. Don't let your guard down!"

With that warning on her mind, Artemis left Athena and set out to find Ares.

Chapter 4

Ares lived in a cave cut deep into the belly of Mount Olympus. Artemis approached the entrance cautiously. She noticed surveillance cameras keeping a watch on the entrance and surrounding area. The opening to the cave was secured with a huge iron gate. She walked up to the gate and searched for a cord to pull or a button to push to announce her arrival. She was startled by a crackle coming over a loudspeaker followed by a stern male voice, "Who goes there?" the voice demanded.

25

"It is Artemis, Goddess of the Hunt," she said cautiously, not knowing to whom she was speaking. "I am here to meet with Ares, God of War. I have been sent by Athena, Goddess of Wisdom."

The loudspeaker crackled again and the voice said, "Your identity must be verified. Open your right hand and place it on the computer monitor to your right. Hold it there for 30 seconds and then wait for processing." Artemis followed the instructions and looked around for a place to sit while she waited. She found a boulder nearby and sat on it. She mused about how strange it was for such a powerful and feared God to go through these extreme measures of security. After waiting for about 12 minutes, Artemis heard some clanking, scratching and squeaking as the mechanisms of the iron gate started to come alive. Slowly a slit appeared in the center of the gate. The slit grew larger and larger as the two great sides of the gate receded into the cave wall.

The loudspeaker crackled once more and the voice said, "Proceed forward down the corridor. You will be greeted when the corridor comes to an end. Don't touch anything!"

Artemis stepped through the door and into a dimly lit hallway. Paintings lined the corridor walls. There were battle scenes of historical wars around the kingdom and around the world. They seemed to be arranged in chronological order with the oldest closest to the entrance. Artemis saw scenes of long ago when people fought with spears and swords. In addition to the paintings, there were ancient weapons displayed in elegant, lighted cases that matched the time period depicted in the paintings. She saw battles with horses and battles on ships. She saw rulers in victory and kings being slain. She saw the emergence of guns and tanks and bombs and she saw death, destruction and misery grow. By the time she reached the end of the corridor she felt the weight of war closing in on her. She felt she would be crushed by the force of destruction that resided in this place. She paused to take a deep breath.

The corridor opened into a large room

that was filled with more war artifacts. It reminded Artemis of a museum. An old man appeared from behind one of the display cases and started slowly walking toward Artemis. His back was bent over almost into a hunch and he looked down at the floor as he shuffled. Although he did not have a limp, he walked with a cane, using it more to keep his balance than anything else. His gray hair was tangled and unkempt. He wore a military uniform of dark blue wool with a cape draped over his shoulders.

"What do you want with me?" he said coldly to Artemis. She looked at him in disbelief. She wondered if this broken man—who looked nothing like the photograph in Athena's book—could really be the great God Ares. He spoke again, responding as if he had heard her thoughts. "You are surprised at my appearance, aren't you? Thought I'd be some powerful Hercules! Strong, virile, fearsome! Is the lady disappointed?" he asked sarcastically. "You came in here for a fight and you're disappointed to find your opponent to be a wretched old man."

"I did not come to fight," Artemis retorted. "I came here to plead with you to release the spell!"

"You can plead all you want—it won't do you a bit of good. The damage has already been done. War is a way of life now. The inhabitants of the world have chosen it. It will destroy them all one day. Destroy them all!" Ares started to wring his hands as he lapsed into thoughts of Earth's demise. He repeated his mantra, "Destroy the soldiers, and the generals and the wives and the little girls and the little boys. Destroy them all! Destroy the horses and the dogs and the cats. Destroy the good and the bad!"

"Stop it!" shouted Artemis. "Stop the destruction! Stop your evil spell!"

"Stop it?" he questioned. "You think I can just wave my hand and undo everything that has happened over centuries?" He laughed. "You naive, stupid girl! I couldn't undo it now if I wanted to! Look at this." He picked up a remote control device and pointed it toward the wall. He pushed one of the control buttons and a giant screen began easing its way down from the ceiling.

Then he pushed another button, this one marked, "Religious." A television picture appeared on the screen.

"What would you like to see?" Ares asked. "The crusades or modern day Catholic/Protestant disputes. How about Muslim vs. Hindu. I can show you gunfire or spears. Bombs or burnings. They are all here." Just then the screen lit up with a great burst of light. The video showed fire erupting everywhere. "This is a good one!" said Ares, turning up the volume. "A bomb blast sets off a fire that kills hundreds. Look at the people run!" Artemis watched as the villagers scattered. Some were already on fire. They screamed in terror and rolled in the dirt to quash the flames. Mangled bodies were strewn about as a result of the blast. Artemis turned away.

"A little too rich for you?" Ares mocked. "Well how about this?" Ares pushed the button marked "Political." The channel on the big screen switched to a scene of two pilots boarding a high tech war plane. They gestured high signs to the ground crew and closed the hatches. Artemis could hear their voices communicating through radio transmissions. They talked about the goals of the mission and intended targets. The men looked young, intelligent and eager to do the job they had been trained to do. They didn't look like killers to Artemis, yet she listened in disbelief as they talked casually about "targets." What they really meant was dropping bombs on cities filled with men, women and children.

"They can't see what they are doing!" she said. "It's the spell that blinds them. You must remove the spell! You must make them stop killing each other. Bring love back!"

"I already told you I can't do that," said Ares. "Look at me! I'm a wretched old man! How do you think I got this way? Being the God of War, that's how! Every single battle that is ever waged on his planet—whether it's a family feud or a nuclear holocaust—falls under my jurisdiction. I must preside over them all!

"When I cast the spell I had no concept of how war would multiply and grow. Now every moment of my day is filled with war. Every dream I have is war! All is war and I

31

am the God of it all! The irony is that it's killing me!"

"There must be a way to stop it," said Artemis. "There must be something to reverse the tide."

"Only one thing," replied Ares. "But it's too late for that now."

"What is it?" demanded Artemis.

"It is love. If love could return to this planet and wash over the entire globe for one full minute, then the spell would begin to break. It wouldn't dissolve completely, but it would be just enough of an infusion of yin to start the process of balance returning to the cosmos. But that cannot happen here. There is too much hate. Even the most sacred institutions like the church and the family are filled with hate. There is no way to bring love back across the planet. It can't happen. War has won! I have won! But the joke's on me. I have won my own extinction! Ha! Ha! Ha!"

Ares' laughter sent a chill up Artemis' spine. He kept on laughing until she could bear it no more. "Let me out of here!" she screamed. Ares did not hear her. He just kept on laughing and laughing. She spotted the remote control lying on the desk. She grabbed it and pushed the button marked "Gate." She ran down the corridor toward the exit and saw the gate opening in front of her. It hesitated momentarily in the open position, then started to close. She ran faster and faster, and slipped through the great slabs of iron the instant before they slammed shut.

Outside of the cave Artemis sat down on the rock and caught her breath. Feeling devastated by the events of the day, she began to weep. "Can't we find just one moment of love? Just one moment!"

Then, something shifted inside of her and she saw the glimmer of an idea. It was an idea of something so powerful that she thought it could unite the world in love—at least for one moment. "Ugh," she sighed. "It might work! But, it will be painful and cruel—to one so undeserving of cruelty!"

Artemis cried out the heavens, "Is there no other way?" The heavens remained silent. She knew what she must do.

Chapter 5

Artemis clothed herself in white flowing fabric and descended like an angel from the heavens into the Princess' kingdom below. On bare feet she crept through the palace until she found the Princess' bedroom. Quietly she opened the door. She knew she need not worry about waking the Prince. The royal couple had long ago adopted separate sleeping quarters.

She saw the Princess sleeping gently. Her head rested softly on a burgundy satin pillowcase. Moonlight streamed through the window, highlighting the Princess' gold-

34

en hair. Artemis paused a moment, awed by the beauty of the scene.

She noticed a trail of dried tears running from the corner of the Princess' eyes into the pillow. Artemis touched the Princess' shoulder and gently called her name. "Do not be afraid, my child," she sang softly. "I am a friend, here to help you."

The Princess awoke and was startled to see an angel singing to her. She was not afraid. The vision of Artemis with the glow of the moon upon her ebony skin was more saintly than threatening.

"Who are you?" the Princess asked.

"I am Artemis, Goddess of the Hunt. It is my duty to make sure fair play is used in hunting and to protect the hunted. I have been watching the hyenas hunt you. They have not been hunting fairly."

The Princess cringed at the thought of the hyenas. "Oh, Artemis, you are right. They torment my soul every day. Can you help me?" she asked. Artemis saw the hope in the Princess' eyes.

"I have tried," said Artemis. "But I have failed. There is a spell cast upon this kingdom that makes it impossible for me to inter-vene. I am so sorry!" Artemis put her arms around the Princess and began to rock her.

The Princess started to cry. The hope she had felt the moment before turned to anguish. "I can't go on any more!" she gulped out the words. "With every move I make the hyenas are there—mocking me, laughing at me, clicking their teeth and snarling.

"I have worked so hard to be a good Princess. I have remade myself over and over again trying to please the Prince, trying to please the people in the kingdom. But it is never enough. They always mock! Why can't they treat me with love? Isn't there any kindness left for me?"

Artemis held back her own tears and steadied her voice. She wanted to be a strong bastion of support for the Princess. "My lady," she said. "My heart breaks just trying to hold some of the pain you feel. But ours aren't the only hearts breaking. There are women all over the world who suffer just like you."

"No!" said the Princess. "It is not possible! No one knows the anguish I feel—the alienation, the isolation. It's like I have been transplanted to this palace from another planet. No one speaks my language. No one cares to learn. They just ridicule me because I am different. I have no one—no one—to go to who will understand me."

"That's exactly it!" exclaimed Artemis. "That's all part of the spell. It's a spell that treats values of the heart as trivial and fair game for ridicule and disdain. All women, all over the world who live by these values—who think in terms of these values—are made to feel stupid and inferior. They cry themselves to sleep at night thinking something is wrong with them. They try to fit in but they can't. They never will as long as the spell has power over the kingdom."

"You mean these women feel just like me—even though their life stories are different?" asked the Princess.

"Yes," said Artemis. "And like you, they blame themselves or their specific circumstances for their pain. One woman cries because her husband left her, another cries over a lost child, another rails out in anger because she was abused as a little girl, another feels she was never loved by her father. Different backgrounds, different stories, common pain. Each woman feels isolated, yet each one's suffering is merely a part of the spell—the spell that has gripped this kingdom into a state of imbalance. The two great cosmic energies of the yin and the yang are no longer in balance. That imbalance keeps the spell in place.

"I don't understand," said the Princess.

"The terms *yin* and *yang*," began Artemis, "are ancient terms that describe energy forces in the universe. The yin is the feminine energy. The yang is the masculine.

"The two are intrinsically equal and dependent on each other. Balance is needed for the world to live in peace and harmony. When there is balance, love emerges as the highest value. When love is the highest value, there is no war, no violence, no poverty. Imagine a kingdom in which all the subjects value love above all things! Just imagine! How would kingdoms and governments run? How would commerce function? What about education, medicine and religion?

"The world would look very different than it looks to you today. Business owners would love their customers and seek to serve them honestly and fairly. They would love their employees and offer them abundance—and their employees would love them back and never take advantage of them. They would work in harmony with their coworkers and resolve differences with love and understanding.

"Religions guided by love would throw out judgement. They would open their arms to all people and give up trying to prove doctrinal correctness. No one would feel the need to be right or superior because a new understanding would emerge that would allow all people to find God in their own way. The rulers of all kingdoms would work toward peace and understanding rather than dominance and war.

"The spell in the kingdom has made it impossible for love to be the highest value because the spell keeps the yin and the yang out of balance. As long as that imbalance exists, love cannot lead."

The Princess considered Artemis' words

carefully. She sat motionless on the corner of her bed, thinking. Then she began to cry. She sobbed for the people in her kingdom who lived in a world without love. She sobbed for the women who have struggled to bring their own yin energy back into balance, but have been thwarted time and time again.

The realization that her pain and her isolation were magnified a million-fold hit her like a violent blow. She let out a wail that echoed across the kingdom. Her wail connected with the pain of all women all over the world and it magnified and grew in strength and intensity. Time stood still for a singular moment as all the pain of the wounded yin coalesced into the Princess' wail.

Artemis watched. Her heart filled with love and admiration for the Princess. She saw that the Princess was a genuine ambassador of love. Artemis put her hands gently on the Princess' shoulder. She sent love, compassion and healing energy to the Princess through her touch. She sang a heavenly lullaby.

The Princess opened her eyes and

asked Artemis, "Is there anything I can do? Can I join you in your mission to end this terrible spell?"

Artemis looked straight into the Princess' blue eyes. "Yes," she said. "There is something. But it is at great cost to you."

The Princess replied, "I am willing."

Artemis told the Princess what would be required of her. The Goddess and the Princess then lowered their voices and devised their plan. Late into the night they talked, sometimes giggling, sometimes crying, sometimes just sitting quietly together. When they had completed their work, the Princess climbed into her bed and Artemis kissed her softly on her forehead. "Good night, sweet child. Thank you for your gift." Artemis tiptoed quietly out of the palace and not a soul knew she had been there.

Chapter 6

The people of the kingdom noticed a change in the Princess. She no longer seemed young and naive. She was a woman coming into her own. She told the Palace to stop controlling her and to let her live her life her own way. She said, "I don't need your guards following me around everywhere. I can take care of myself."

The people of the kingdom said she was a rose opening up to its fullness—beautiful, fragrant and becoming aware of her own power. On a summer evening a few weeks after Artemis had visited her, the

Princess left the Palace for a walk around the royal estate. The sky was pink and the air fragrant with the sweetness of the last days of summer. The Princess felt light-hearted and happy. She knew now that happily-ever-after would never come from her Prince. It would come from the depths of her own soul. She was beginning to understand how the descent she had made into her own despair was a necessary part of her rebirth into her fullness as a woman.

These thoughts filled her mind as she turned down a winding pathway. It was lined on one side with lush vegetation and on the other side was a lazy creek. The path continued underneath a bridge and then opened out into a garden of roses. The Princess proceeded under the bridge and savored the cool dampness of the shaded area. As she emerged from the bridge into the garden, she decided to sit for a while on a nearby bench amidst the beauty and fragrance of the roses. The roses were arranged in the colors of the rainbow, graduating in subtle hues of red, orange, yellow, green, blue, indigo and violet. As soon as the

Princess sat down on the bench a hyena bounded out from the bushes toward her. She screamed, jumped up and started to run back toward the bridge.

"Haw! Haw! Haw!" clicked the Hyena. "Run, Princess! We're right on your heals!" Six more hyenas jumped out from behind the bushes and joined the leader in his pursuit. They all clicked their tongues, snarled and laughed. "Run, Princess, run!"

She ran with all her might and made it to the bridge. As she stepped into the shaded area, her foot slipped on a rock and she fell into the creek. She struggled to stand up, but before she could get fully upright the lead hyena pounced upon her, throwing her hard against the embankment. The other hyenas were right behind the first. They jumped on the Princess, pinned her down and tore at her clothes and her flesh. The lead hyena laughed a loud, hideous laugh and plunged his long teeth into her throat. The Princess gasped, raised her eyes toward the heavens and whispered her last words, "May the spell be broken!"

Chapter 7

News of the Princess' death traveled around the world in little more than an instant. Every television station and every radio station, in every language announced, "The Princess is Dead!" A stunned world did not know how to react. They just watched. They stared at the images coming across the television screen and tried to make sense out of them. Women were especially captivated—women like Sarah Deerborn who lived in a remote part of the kingdom. She watched in disbelief and sadness.

Sarah sat in front of her television, mesmerized by the events that unfolded before her. She was surprised at her own interest as she was not a follower of the royal family. Usually she didn't like watching television much at all, but she couldn't tear herself away from this event. She felt connected to it in some way that she could not explain. Her husband criticized her saying, "Haven't you had enough of that?" But Sarah hadn't had enough. She kept watching and watching.

On the day of the Princess' funeral Sarah set her alarm clock for the early morning hours so she could get up and watch it live on television. She slid out of bed and went into the television room with her fuzzy slippers and comforter. She sat on the floor and lit a candle. She watched the crowds line the streets and saw how the men, women and children brought flowers and lit candles in loving tribute to the Princess.

Sarah listened to the sounds of the clip, clop of the horses as they pulled the flag-draped casket down the street. She heard the drone of the church bells in the distance and the sobs of the crowd. Occasionally a mourner would wail out with a burst of sobs or call out the Princess' name.

Above it all, Sarah heard the voices of the television commentators. On and on they went, analyzing the life of the Princess, her marriage, her role as mother, her work, her passions, her pain. They eulogized her and they canonized her and they puzzled over the huge outpouring of love that was coming her way. They had never seen such a wave of loss and heartbreak swelling up over the kingdom and the world. They pondered, "was it because she was a beautiful Princess?" But they sensed there was more to it than that. They discussed how she never quite fit into the royal family. She was a woman of heart, caring and passion. The royals were stoic—bound by duty, rules and protocol.

The television reporters knew the Princess was different, but because of the spell they could not quite see why. They couldn't see that she was the yin personified. She was the archetypal feminine, full of compassion and grace and nurturing and

47

motherhood. They couldn't see why she didn't fit—and could never fit, no matter how hard she tried. The people of her kingdom had agreed long, long ago to accept the power of the spell. They agreed as a whole culture to submit to the social hypnosis that the yin is inferior to the yang, the feminine inferior to the masculine and the Princess less valuable than the Prince. Because of the spell, no one could see that the Princess *had to die*. She could not live in this world because this world despised her.

Nonetheless, even under the spell everyone seemed to wake up to a feeling of loss. They felt a huge void left by the Princess' departure. They didn't value her in life because the spell made her appear valueless. But after her death, they felt the vacuum left by her absence.

"Who can take her place?" the people cried. "Who will be our Queen of Hearts now?" The television commentators echoed the cries. "Who will fill the void left by the Princess?"

Sarah watched and listened in the darkness of the early morning hours. Her candle flickered and she started to repeat the mantra of the day, "Who will fill the void? Who will fill the void?" Over and over she uttered the words. Then she picked up her drum, closed her eyes and started to tap out the sound of her own heartbeat.

Louder and louder she played as she sang out the question, "Who will fill the void?" Her drumbeat continued and she rocked forward and backward. She felt primitive in her power, somehow connected to the wisdom of the ancients. "Who will fill the void?" She sang aloud and then deep from her gut came a reply: "I will."

Still drumming and rocking, she began repeating her new mantra, "I will. I will. I will!" In a trance-like state Sarah drummed and called out her commitment to the cosmos. "I will!" As she continued, women around the kingdom began to feel the heartbeat and hear the words. "I will!" They picked up their drums and maracas and started to sing and dance and play. "I will," they sang. "I will!"

At first there were just a handful of women joining in and then more and more came until there were a hundred, then a thousand and then a million all singing of love and seeing hope for the first time.

As Sarah kept drumming the veil of the spell was lifted from her eyes. She saw the way the world had been and how the spell had created imbalance. She saw how war and poverty and hunger and violence, all the ills of society—could be traced to this imbalance. Then she saw a vision of how it could be changed, of how the spell could be broken throughout the kingdom.

She set down her drum, picked up her pen and began to write in her journal.

I have a vision...

I see a world very different from the world I live in. It is a world that honors the yin and values it as equal to the yang.

I see a sixteen year old girl who is unmarried and pregnant who doesn't have to choose between a life of shameful poverty and abortion. She knows she will be welcomed into a circle of women where she will learn to bring forth her gifts.

I see a world that honors the sexuality of all women, in its many diverse manifestations, and recognizes it as sacred and beautiful.

I see a world where a woman doesn't feel economic need to stay with a husband who beats her, because she knows she will be welcomed into a circle of women who will help her to find her voice and her gifts.

I see a new mother who doesn't have to choose between staying home with her baby and going back to work. I see a world that incorporates children into the workplace so a woman does not have to make a choice between being marginalized as a homemaker and being taken seriously as a career woman.

I see education pulled out of the hands of the sun gods and given back to the Goddess of Wisdom. I see the process for teaching becoming less like a banker depositing knowledge on students and becoming more like a midwife drawing the knowledge out of each individual learner.

I see a political structure that values the yin—values nurturing and non-violence and Earth and no longer feels the need to conquer, dominate and control the sensitivity and truth that the Goddess brings.

I see a medical system that honors the medicine woman. It values the natural healing wisdom of our bodies and gives up the ego need to "cure."

51

I see these things and I long to help them manifest themselves in our world today. Then I see a way. I see the way the great leader from history, Mohandas Gandhi, freed his country from the rule of tyrants, and I see a parallel of how we can free the yin from the tyranny of the yang—with non-violence and with wisdom.

Gandhi's people felt helpless to do anything about their enslavement because the kingdom that enslaved them had the wealth and the power and the weapons. Similarly, women feel powerless to rise up against the strength of the patriarchy because it holds the positions of power—and has all the weapons.

But Gandhi helped his people see that each individual has power. He cried out against the products of his country's oppressors. He helped his people see that they were supporting their oppressors with their own money. Once they realized they no longer needed these products and started making their own, a shift occurred and the great powers took note.

So it is with the world today. Women buy into the vision that the yang culture has for us. We support it with our dollars. Marketers know that most buying decisions are made by women.

All the industries that are killing us are supported by us.

We have tremendous power. We have economic power. We can reclaim it by turning away from our insatiable desire to have more and more of what is offered to us by the yang. We think it will fill up the void inside us, but it enslaves us instead. We can start to reclaim our power by creating circles of women rippling out everywhere, helping women discover the void is filled from within, not without. Women will come to know that they don't need a closet full of clothes, or a house full of things. They will learn what is enough.

And they will crave to purchase the things they need from women, like them, who have found their grounding in the yin. Women can create small industries and they will be able to compete with the big businesses because they will be supported by their sisters and the power of the yin will bless them.

We can learn to say "no" to the products that are made by our tyrants. We can build cooperatives and networks. Quietly and gently an infrastructure will grow that supports itself. The big corporations will no longer be needed to sustain us. We will no longer sustain them.

Gradually, as the money flow slows down to the big yang industries, the powers that be will start to notice. They will rage at us. They will want to burn us—and some of us may die along the way.

They cannot stop us. The yin is returning. I hope I can be part of preparing the way for her.

As Sarah completed the words tears pooled up in her eyes and began to fall upon the pages. They fell in colors. First red then orange then yellow, green, blue, indigo and finally violet. As the colors poured out of her, her mind became clearer and clearer as if a great cloak of deception had been removed. She saw her vision with crystal clarity and she was amazed by it. The words and concepts seemed strange to her and she marveled that they had been written by her own hand. It excited her to think that such a revolution could really take place and that Earth could be healed. She prayed that it would come to pass.

Chapter 8

The next day Sarah received a troubling telephone call. It was her 16-year-old niece Mindy with news that she was going to have a baby. Mindy sobbed into the phone, "What can I do? What can I do?" Sarah could feel the agony of Mindy's position. She seemed to have very few choices. Marriage was not one of them. The father of the child was barely older than Mindy and not capable of supporting a family. Mindy could choose to raise the child on her own, but she had no means of support. The job market for an untrained, uneducated and inexperienced teenager was not promising. She would likely need financial assistance from the government. Another choice was putting the baby up for adoption, but she feared that could haunt her for life. Abortion loomed as the third option, but that, too, could create a life-long scar.

Sarah contemplated another choice. Could it be possible to create a circle of feminine support for Mindy? Support like she had seen in her vision? Sarah decided it was worth a try.

Sarah talked with her friend Anne. She showed her the vision she had written on the night of the Princess' funeral. "Can you see this vision too?" she asked.

"Yes! I can see it!" said Anne. She began to cry the colorful tears of awakening that Sarah had shed the night she had written the vision. Tears came and came. First red, then orange, yellow, green, blue, indigo and violet.

One by one Sarah showed the vision to her friends and their response was always the same. Rivers of tears in the beautiful colors of the rainbow. Sarah marveled at the magic and felt a powerful force of change. The insidious spell that had plagued the Princess was beginning to break into fragments. As woman after woman experienced an awakening, the spell became weaker and weaker.

The women wanted to be part of a circle like the one Sarah had described in her vision. Some wanted to share in the power of feminine energy—breathing in and out the life force of the yin. Others, like Sandy and Nancy, needed the circle for very specific healing. Sandy was a single mother of five-year-old Jason. Her former husband undermined her as a mother and toyed with his child's tender, vulnerable emotions. Sandy felt powerless as she saw her son's confusion. She feared the confusion would become in Jason the same rage that consumed his father. She felt a desperate need for support.

Nancy was a working mom who loved her work—and her family. She had worked hard to earn her credentials as a physician and now that her practice was thriving, she found her work rewarding, yet demanding.

She craved balance. She hoped the circle would help her to find her center—an anchor to keep her from being torn to pieces by all the forces that pulled at her.

Some of the women in the circle were teen mothers or pregnant like Mindy. Others were in their family-raising years, and others, like Sarah, were older with no children at home. It was a good blend of backgrounds, needs and dreams—with one common desire—that the circle could help them heal the woundedness they had felt and return to them a true grounding in the feminine yin.

Thirteen women assembled at the group's first gathering. They sat crossed-legged on the floor of Sarah's large living room. She had moved the furniture to make space for everyone. As the women settled into their spots on the floor, a hush fell over the room. They sat for several minutes in silence. Sarah lit a candle and held it up in front of her. "I will introduce myself in a ceremonial fashion, recognizing my feminine lineage," she said. "I am Sarah, daughter of Mary, granddaughter of Emma and Hazel, great granddaughter of Gertrude and Elizabeth."

She passed the candle to her right and Sandy said, "I am Sandy, daughter of Janet, granddaughter of Tess and Rachel, great-granddaughter of Abigail and Florence, mother of Emily." Sandy passed the candle to Mindy and Mindy to Heather and Heather to Melanie until every woman announced her presence in the circle in the same way. When the candle returned to Sarah, she set it on the floor in front of her and they all sat in silence again. The silence grew and enveloped them like a soft comforter draped around shivering shoulders. They had all unknowingly been shivering emotionally due to the cold indifference they had felt living in a kingdom under a spell. The silence comforted them, slowly bringing to their consciousness a feeling of safety—permission to just *be*—no requirement to rush about and accomplish things—but to just be.

The women learned how to speak into the silence. This was a different kind of speaking than they had done before.

Speaking into the silence meant releasing their pain. As one woman spoke, the other women heard and acknowledged, but did not need to respond or offer "helpful" solutions. Instead, the women of the circle let the silence answer. It answered by becoming a container to hold the pain. It didn't wash it away. It didn't pretend it didn't exist. It just held it, and honored it, and in so doing, it eased the suffering of the women who had felt they were required to hold it all by themselves.

Mindy was the first to speak. "I don't know what to do about this baby," she said, placing her hands on her abdomen. "I want to be a good mom, but how can I? I don't have money to support a child and I don't have a job. I haven't even finished high school!" Tears began to stream down her cheeks and her words came out in little gulps. "I feel so helpless and trapped. Sometimes I wish my baby would just go away and die. Then I hate myself for wishing it. I think it would be better if *I* died!"

Sarah watched as the women in the circle witnessed Mindy's pain. The silence felt uncomfortable at first. Shouldn't someone respond, or offer comfort or advice? Instead everyone remained silent. Mindy spoke again. "I really want this baby," she said. "I want to love it and I want it to love me. I want to do everything for it. We will have a special bond—a bond like I have with no one else on Earth. I want that. I want to love and be loved so much!"

Again the women were silent. Mindy began to cry fully now. Sandy handed her a box of tissues and the tears kept coming, "I just don't know what to do," she sobbed. "I don't know what to do!"

Sarah gently touched her face and moved her light brown hair away from her eyes. She wanted to help Mindy in a real way. Not just with words, but with power. "Would you like us to surround you and offer you our healing energy?" she asked.

Mindy looked up with a puzzled expression. "Okay," she said hesitantly. "But I'm not sure what that means."

Sarah took her hand and said, "Come to the center of the circle." Mindy sat down in the center of the circle and Sarah sat next to her, then motioned to the other women to come in closer and surround Mindy. Sarah placed her hands on Mindy's knee. The other women followed her lead. Some scooted over and placed their hands on Mindy's crossed legs and feet. Others moved into kneeling position and put their hands on Mindy's shoulders. Sandy and Melanie stood up and leaned across the other women to place their hands on Mindy's head. For minutes they stayed there, touching Mindy, summoning their healing power and the feminine wisdom of the ages. They created a gap in time where they brought a coalescing of yin energy to soothe and comfort Mindy and to begin the healing process. They stayed with Mindy until they felt a sense of completeness. Then they returned to their places in the circle, allowing the silence to envelop them once more.

Anne spoke next. She looked young for her 43 years. Her hair was still dark brown and shiny with only a few strands of gray. The other women attributed her youthful appearance to the carefree life she led. She and her husband enjoyed two incomes and no children to be responsible for. They were free to travel, pursue art and hobbies. Anne's life appeared to be the ultimate care-free adventure. But to Anne, her life felt quite different. "I want to apologize to the group," she said. "As Mindy was speaking, I found my mind filled with resentful—almost hateful—thoughts. I do not want to bring this ugliness to the group."

"I apologize for feeling so judgmental toward Mindy. I guess I am feeling resentful and jealous that she is being allowed to have what I was not. I have always wanted to have a child, but I know now that I never will."

Anne paused, breathed deeply and looked at the floor. "It's not for lack of opportunity. When I was 16, just like Mindy, I was pregnant. But unlike her, I chose not to have the baby. I had an abortion. It's hard for me to even say that. The irony is that I *wanted* to have that baby so much. All of my life I wanted to have a baby of my own. I don't know where it came from, but I know it was a strong desire inside me.

"When the time came that it was actually possible for me to have a baby, it wasn't like I had imagined at all. There were no baby showers, no excitement, no encouragement—just a 'problem' I needed to solve. My parents helped me to see that the only solution was to terminate the pregnancy. So I went away to another part of the country and had a surgical procedure that was described to me as, 'No more difficult than having a tooth pulled.'

"In a few days I returned to school and to all the world I was a normal teenager again. No one knew my secret. But I knew— I knew something had changed. There was no longer a baby growing inside of me, instead a new self-concept had been conceived. I have come to think of that self-concept as *The Anti-Mother*. Unbeknownst to me, *The Anti-Mother* began to take over my life. She guided me further and further away from having children by planting in me a knowing that I would be an awful mother. On a deep level I feared that I was not a nurturer of children; I was a killer of them. Even though on the surface I desperately wanted children, I continued to make

64

decisions in my life that kept me away from them. The wrong men, the wrong timing, the wrong financial setting. Time went by. Years went by. Still I hoped it was not too late for me.

"But *The Anti-Mother* had prevailed. Even though I now have all the trappings of the perfect environment for a baby—a stable marriage, a nice home, health insurance, new car—now my body won't allow it. For too many years I have been living, breathing and manifesting *The Anti-Mother*. Every cell of my body believes it now."

Anne began to cry. "They say abortion is murder," she said, "But, for me it has been suicide. A long, slow, silent painful death. I don't know how to stop it." She lowered her head into her hands and began to cry harder. She cried for her loss, her pain and her emptiness. She cried for the hole she felt inside her. Her sobs grew longer and deeper and primitive. Her pain became the pain of all women, all generations, all creatures who have had their motherhood ripped from them. The weight of the pain filled the room and all the women in the circle began to wail. They wailed together for several minutes, offering deep, guttural cries of anguish up to the heavens. Their voices grew louder and softer in unison as if responding to an ancient rhythm.

Gradually the keening subsided and the women circled around Anne to provide a cocoon of love and security. They touched her and spoke softly to her, reassuring her. She felt embarrassed and afraid they would judge her and condemn her as she had done to herself for so many, many years. But, they just held her in the balm of love.

Day after day the women met in the circle. Each woman in her own time brought her story forward into the silence. Every woman gave birth to her own anguish and the silence held it carefully, without judgement. As each woman shared, she was surrounded by the others and received their powerful healing energy. Karen told how her husband had abandoned her. Traci told of the abuse she had suffered as a child. Connie shared how she'd spent her life trying to win her mother's approval and Melanie grieved the loss of her son.

Teri had been shy about speaking into the silence. Her story didn't seem as important or urgent as the others. Her childhood years had been happy. Her parents loved her and encouraged her. They taught her that she could accomplish anything she set her mind to. No one was surprised that she graduated from high school with honors, went on to one of the best colleges and married a handsome young man with a promising career. Her own career was progressing nicely, too. She had rapidly worked her way up through the ranks of a major advertising firm to become an account executive. Recently, however, she had left her job to stay at home with her nine-month-old daughter.

She opened up to the circle on the day her company announced her replacement for the job. "I don't know quite what I want to say," she started. "I just feel upset about being 'replaced' at my company. I don't know why it's bothering me. I know I made the right decision to stay home with Brittany. I know she needs her mother—and I love being a mother. It's not that I'm jealous either. I know the woman they promoted to take my place and she'll do a great job. I'm excited for her. But I just can't help feeling that a door has closed for me.

"I've worked hard at my career. I have always gotten a lot of positive feedback and my self-esteem was feeling pretty solid. Then I had Brittany and everything changed. I intended to keep working after she was born—I even went back to work after three months of maternity leave. It was unbearable to leave her at the day care each day. From the depths of my soul a voice called out to me, 'Don't leave that child! You are her mother! That is the most sacred bond!'

"I thought after time it might get easier, but it never did. One day I was at my mother's house and her friend Alice dropped by. Alice works at a corporate job as an administrative assistant. She went back to work about five years ago after spending twenty years at home raising her two children. The three of us were having a conversation about kids and jobs and this and that. I mentioned how hard it had been for me to juggle my mothering life with my career. Alice chimed in, 'Well Honey, you're doing the right thing by going back to work. I can't tell you how many times I wish I hadn't stayed home. Just think of where I could be now if I hadn't wasted all those years at home with my kids!'

"When Alice uttered those words about 'wasting' years, something clicked inside of me. How could she say that about motherhood? She was willing to throw away the most sacred trust ever given to her—that of two human lives. I looked at my own life and felt sick. I turned in my notice at work the next day.

"But staying home has been harder than I thought it would be. I no longer get lauded for a job well done. There's no one to tell me my work is important. In fact, it is just the opposite. It seems that everywhere I look I get messages from the culture that tell me that the really important work in this world is the kind you get *paid* for. Raising kids just gets in the way.

"I also recognize that it is only because I am married that I even have the luxury to stay home from work and be a full-time mom. That doesn't feel right to me either. I keep thinking about Sarah's vision of women working day in and day out with children at their sides. Why is this world so disconnected from that? Why is the desire of my heart so foreign to the way things work? What's wrong with me? What's wrong with our culture?"

Teri let go a flood of tears she had been holding inside. She cried into the silence and let it hold her pain. After some time passed, Sarah asked Teri what the group could do for her. Teri responded by requesting validation. "I need to know that my work is important." Sarah guided the women to circle around Teri and each one, in turn, made a loving statement to her:

"You are a wonderful mother—and that is the most important job in the world."

"Your daughter is very fortunate to have you teaching her what it means to grow into a woman."

"You are a beautiful role model."

"Bless you for recognizing Brittany's need for you—and for having the courage and strength to be there for her."

When all the accolades had been spoken, Teri sat in the center and received healing touch from the women. The power of the yin flowed through her, nourishing her deep feminine need.

As weeks went by the women could see something magic was happening in the group. One day Nancy told how it was affecting her. "I have been thinking about our group and how different it is than anything I've experienced before. It feels like I'm at home here, like I belong. I have been an alien wandering this planet and finally I've found a place where I fit. When Sarah invited me to this group I was skeptical. I have seen a war going on between women and I didn't see how we could get past it. The battle lines are drawn deep in our psyches. We fear younger, slimmer and prettier women—women who will steal our men. We fear rich women, powerful women and tough women. We fear women bosses and women leaders. We fear women who are different from us. Even though I know in my heart that this is a battle that should never be fought, I couldn't see a way to overcome such deep social conditioning. At first, even I felt a little distant from the rest of the group. But I stuck with it and gradually I began to gain a new understanding.

Our stories are different and we all play different roles in this world—but our feminine natures are the same. Our need to connect with that feminine is what unites us. When we come together in honesty and openness; we are powerful. We can heal the wounds. We can heal the world!"

Chapter 9

Sarah watched the power of the group grow and she was awed by it. She listened to the stories the women told and saw how they all pointed to the same thing. Each woman revealed a profound sense of unworthiness. This unworthiness was so deep and so ingrained that no amount of counseling or therapy or drugs could get rid of it. It existed in the cellular memory of each woman—planted there by generations and generations of women living in a world that has told them they are unworthy. Sarah wondered how the lives of

73

all women might have been different if they had heard since birth an affirmation of their beauty and their value and their deep worthiness. She wondered how the whole world might have been different if it had not been cast under the shadow of the spell.

Sarah took her leadership role in the circle very seriously. She had spent much of her time during the months since the first meeting organizing, planning and meditating. She didn't have time to read the newspaper, watch television or keep up with the local gossip. One day she happened into the television room while her husband was watching. An advertisement for a weight loss product came across the screen. Sarah saw a beautiful slim woman touting the virtues of the product. It took just a quick glimpse of it to make Sarah feel as if she had been kicked. "Wow!" she thought. "For months I have been affirmed and reaffirmed by women who care about me. I have been feeling good about myself and learning to accept myself just as I am. Then 60 seconds of television and I'm back to doubting myself and feeling like there is something about me that needs to be fixed. My hips are too big, my breasts too small. I never realized how powerful those images are."

Sarah took her new insight back to the group. The women's eyes were opened to the power that the negative images have over them. They couldn't see this before because the spell had blinded them. But now it was clear. They saw how television, fashion magazines and "beauty" products attempt to force them into some false ideal of beauty. The "ideal" figure is a mere skeleton—without the soft round curves so natural to womanhood. The "fashionable" clothes are designed to be worn by this ideal. Advertisements feature it. Movies glamorize it. Young women are literally dying to achieve it by creating eating disorders. As the women in the group discussed how the fashion industry has exploited them, Mindy blurted out, "I'm never going to buy clothes again!"

"Be realistic," countered Melanie. "We can't stop wearing clothes!"

"No we can't." said Mindy, "But what if we started making our own?"

"Yes!" agreed Sandy. "We could design clothes that would honor our bodies and respect our natural curves. Clothes that won't pinch us at the waist and make us suck in our stomachs. Clothes that will be beautiful and flowing and full of grace. Something a Goddess would wear!"

"Perfect!" exclaimed Connie. "We can call it 'Goddesswear'!"

That was the beginning of a new, exciting project for the women of the circle. Sandy and Melanie designed the patterns. Teri found the fabric, and Mindy, Anne and Megan sewed the pieces together. Beautiful embroidery was stitched by Sarah, and Nancy added traditional beadwork.

At the next meeting of the circle the women celebrated by wearing their new "Goddesswear." Some wore dresses, some slacks. Mindy's yellow maternity dress was particularly beautiful. It honored her body and the new shape it was taking on. The women sat in the circle looking around to see the soft, simple beauty of their creation. They smiled and entered the silence in awesome gratitude.

As time went on the group continued to make more clothes. Sandy, Mindy, Melanie and Sarah were putting the most time into it because they didn't have outside jobs to consume their time. Friends requested special orders. Then friends of friends asked for orders. Goddesswear was becoming a small industry.

Sarah saw how her vision was beginning to come true. Women were supporting each other and turning away from the industries that devalued them. Sarah began to speak to women's groups around the kingdom. She told of the spell and how it was beginning to crumble. She told of the circle and the power of feminine energy when it is allowed to coalesce. She told of the tyranny of this culture and how women need to join together to support each other to rise out of poverty and the prevailing feeling of unworthiness. She told Mindy's story—a young girl about to become a mother without any support system. She told of Mindy's choices. She could go on welfare, or she could take a minimum wage job and let her baby be raised in day care.

"But," Sarah asked, "how might Mindy's life be different if she could use her creativity and talents to create Goddesswear while raising her child at home? You can help Mindy, and women like her by consciously making an effort to purchase what they create. They are not asking for donations or welfare. They just need us to receive with love what they have created with love. It's a small price to pay to welcome the yin back into this world."

If the spell had still been in full force, the women would not have been able to see the wisdom in Sarah's words. Instead they would have questioned why they should care for Mindy—after all Mindy had gotten herself into trouble. It wasn't their responsibility. They would have quibbled about the price of Goddesswear and decided to spend their money where they could buy things cheaper, or where they could get a big designer name.

That's not the way they saw it now. They could see that they were just like Mindy—connected to her woundedness. They knew that by helping Mindy heal, they were helping themselves and they were creating a shift in the collective consciousness. They ordered Goddesswear for themselves, for their daughters, for their mothers, sisters and friends. The Goddesswear business grew to a comfortable size that supported the three women from the circle who worked at it full time. Sandy, Mindy and Melanie sewed daily, yet they were not consumed by the business. They brought love into their work and love guided them to care for themselves and their children and to be wary of seeking production and profit as higher values than love. They sewed their love into the clothes they made, singing songs of blessings for their customers who would wear them.

Sarah continued to travel around the kingdom sharing the message of the circle and the power of the yin. Women began to start circles in their communities. They asked Sarah for guidance. "How do we organize the circle? How do we create our own yin industries? Where do we go from here?" Sarah heard their requests and decided to create a school to teach them. She built it with the help of her husband and friends from the circle. Women came from far and wide to learn how to heal the wounded yin in their own lives, reclaim their feminine spirit and manifest their creativity by producing something of value for others. They learned how to sew and weave and embroider and bead and spin fibers into fabrics.

They learned how to create yin industries of all types: clothing, food, jewelry, shoes, pottery and ceramics—even furniture. They merged their talents with love and soon their products were sought around the land.

Children were central to Sarah's school. They played and sang and brought their delightful creative energy into the process of learning and working. Women learned how to use that energy to aid the holistic creative process. Children weren't shushed and shoved aside, they were given important roles to play as part of the process.

The women learned how to make love their highest value. When they completed their studies at the school and went back into their own communities, they were committed to their new value system. They shared it in their homes, their schools and their churches.

Gradually things in the kingdom began to change. Women learned they could support themselves and that they did not need to be dependent on toxic jobs and dependency-creating welfare systems. Yin industries sprang up all over the kingdom and were supported by women and men who had emerged from under the spell. As the economic base began to shift, the yang industries began to notice. Some got very, very angry and railed against the women, saying they were destroying the financial future of the kingdom. They called them radicals and troublemakers and witches and thieves. But their naysaying could not stop the powerful force that was spreading across the kingdom. The spell that had kept the yin dominated by the yang for so many centuries was now in fragments and the balance was returning to the universe. More and more people—both men and women— began to recognize the importance of this balance and they honored it by their actions.

Giant corporations that had been power and profit driven in the past began to re-evaluate themselves. They started to recognize the interconnectedness of all things and how their pursuit of progress and dominance had added to the imbalance that was destroying peace and harmony in the world. They knew they needed to bring the yin values of love, compassion, caring and intuition back into their culture. They learned how to make decisions differently. Instead of asking, "How will we profit?" they asked, "What would love do?"

Workplaces began to look much different. Children were invited to participate instead of being shunted aside. They were valued for their energy, creativity and spirit. Children's centers were found in companies all over the kingdom. Young boys and girls were invited to creative meetings, important luncheons and they often sat alongside their parents as they worked. Parents no longer felt the chasm between their work lives and their home lives. Mothers no longer needed to choose between a career where they would be taken seriously and staying home where they would be trivialized by a culture that saw child rearing as a lesser job. Some people had feared that productivity and progress would suffer terribly by having children around, but they found that it did not because they had discovered a new way to channel children's energy. Parents were happier and more productive because they were near their children. Children grew up feeling more secure and more loved. As they grew into young adults and began to enter the workforce themselves, they were positive forces for good. A change had occurred, and instead of generation after generation becoming more and more dysfunctional, the condition started to reverse. The generations became more and more balanced and full of love.

As love grew, the people in the kingdom began to have new insights into racial and religious differences. They could see that love would embrace all the diversity in color and in thought. They opened their arms and embraced one another and with each embrace love grew and multiplied. In the bright light of love, violence could not survive. One man took his gun and laid it down in the Palace rose garden where the Princess had been killed so many years before. It was a gesture recognizing the peace the Princess had brought into this world as well as his own promise to disavow violence. The people of the kingdom were moved by his act and others started to follow his lead. They brought handguns and rifles, knives and chains, clubs and pipes. People brought them day after day. The Palace guards didn't know what to do with the weapons, so they stored them under lock and key on the Palace grounds.

A new relationship with Earth emerged in the kingdom. People began to value the gifts of Mother Earth. They honored her and realized that to live in love meant replenishing the Earth and not emptying her of all the resources she has to give. They learned to say "enough" and not always press to take more and more. They learned to ask permission of Mother Earth and ask how their taking would affect generations to come. Mother Earth began to respond to this new outpouring of concern for her. She started to heal and her garden become more vibrant and alive every day.

Year after year the women of the circle grew older. Their daughters joined in the group and then their granddaughters. The older women entered the new role of wise crone—and their wisdom was respected. Younger women learned how to use their intuition, to honor their feelings and how to seek their own inner feminine voice.

They lit candles, offered healing touch, danced and beat drums together. Their music resonated with the harmony of the universe. They celebrated the return of the yin, and soon all of the kingdom began to celebrate as well.

Chapter 10

By and by at the Palace, the Prince who had swept the Princess off her feet so long ago, became King. He ruled the land for thirty years and witnessed sweeping changes taking place as the world emerged from under the spell. He often felt unprepared to deal with these changes, as the yin had always been a mystery to him. He wondered how his life might have been different if he had recognized the beauty and worthiness of his wife during her lifetime. Would he have been able to protect her from death? Would she have been able to help him cope with this strange new world?

As the King aged and became more and more frail, the people began to wonder about his successor to the throne. Prince Nathaniel was the heir apparent, but the people were wary and unsure of him. After his mother's death, the royal family had taken special precautions to protect Nathaniel from the public eye. He grew into a young man, and still he kept his distance from public life. He refused official duties and spent his time in study and meditations.

It was a gray spring morning when the palace bells tolled out the announcement of the King's death. The people of the kingdom mourned his passing and came out to honor him at a lavish royal funeral. He had been a good king, but somehow he never endeared himself to his people in a personal way. He was respected and honored, but not adored.

As time passed, the people of the kingdom turned their thoughts toward their new King, Nathaniel. It was customary in the kingdom for a new king to be installed to the throne at a coronation ceremony. The people expected this and looked forward to it. They started to worry when the Palace failed to announce a date. Days went by, then weeks, and still the Palace was silent. The only activity anyone saw was in the rose garden. The people saw backhoes and trucks and people coming in and out of the garden. They couldn't imagine what was going on. "King Nathaniel is insane!" they cried. "He will be the ruin of this kingdom!"

Finally, the flow of people and vehicles into the garden grew to a trickle and then stopped altogether. Curiosity seekers tried to peer through the fence, but they couldn't see anything except an unusual tent-like structure in the center. It measured about 25 feet long, 20 feet wide and only three feet high. People wondered what business the Palace had with a miniature tent. Then the announcement came. The coronation of King Nathaniel Paul would be held in the garden on the second Saturday of July.

The kingdom was abuzz with anticipation on the day of the big event. People flocked to the Palace grounds, hoping to get a place inside the garden once the gates were opened. Television crews perched on scaffolds, on rooftops and hovered above in helicopters. It was as if the entire country held its breath, waiting for a glimpse of the new King and a hint of the leadership he would bring to the kingdom.

Sarah Deerborn made the long trip across the kingdom to attend the coronation. She had recently celebrated her 83rd birthday and was slowing down somewhat. She spent her days peacefully reading, meditating and looking in on the school. She led a class now and then, but had turned operating responsibilities over to her niece Mindy. Mindy was a special joy to Sarah. She had grown into a mature wise woman who had raised a lovely daughter in the ways of the yin.

Sarah's friends advised her against embarking on such a long trip, saying it would be too much for her. Sarah was undaunted. She felt a calling to attend the coronation ceremony and she had learned long ago to respond to such callings.

She arrived at the palace early on the day of the event. Even in the hustle and bustle of the crowd, she managed to get around quite well. She was grateful for the kindness of the people there. Strangers respected her age and were protective of her in her frailty.

An entourage of royal guards opened the garden gates at precisely 1:30 p.m. People flooded into the grounds and circled around the miniature tent. A kind gentleman assisted Sarah to a seat in the garden. The fragrance of roses created a soothing aura of peacefulness. The chaos of the crowd began to quiet and settle into a soft receptiveness. They waited eagerly, but not impatiently, for the new king to appear. At 2 p.m. Nathaniel's carriage arrived. He emerged and stepped up to the podium. Without introduction the King began his address.

"Welcome! It is a momentous day. You have come to witness a coronation and a coronation you shall see! As a prelude to that, I would like to share my philosophy with you and how I came to be the man I am today.

"Forty years ago my mother died in this garden. That event changed the course of my life, and perhaps the course of history. The people of the world poured out their grief and love for her after she was gone. The wave of affection was overpowering—a force of love like this world had never seen. It truly was a glorious time.

"But I was blind to the glory. I was a teenage boy devastated by the loss of my mother. The outpouring of love for her did not help. It only made me angry. I couldn't help but feel that if people had shown her that love while she was alive, maybe she would not have died.

"My anger grew into hatred. I hated the hyenas who killed her. I hated a culture that allowed them to stalk her and I hated myself for the wretched man I was becoming.

"I even hated the citizen of this kingdom who made a gesture of peace by laying his weapon here in honor of my mother. I wanted to shake him and scream at him. 'Don't you see! Your gesture is meaningless! One small amount of peace cannot survive in this world. Hate will devour you—just like it devoured my mother!'

"Every day I walked through this garden and I saw more and more weapons appear. Each one was another testament of a growing consciousness of love and peace. A great shift was occurring in the cosmos. It started like an Earthquake on the day of my mother's death and rippled out in after-shocks since then. My anger so consumed me that I could not see what was happening.

"Then, during one of my walks through the garden I saw an unusually large arsenal of weapons left by well-meaning peace lovers. I became enraged. I was tired of collecting the weapons of the world. I kicked against the stack of weapons and screamed in pain. A hidden knife had sliced through my shoe and into the soft skin between my toes. I limped to the bench to remove my shoe and survey the damage. Blood soaked my stocking and as I removed it, my blood dripped in big red drops onto the ground. I thought it ironic that my blood should spill in this place where my mother had spilled hers.

"I held my foot in pain, summoning the courage to limp out of the garden to call for help. Before I could rise, I felt a hand on my shoulder. I looked and saw no one there, but I felt the powerful presence of my mother. I could hear her voice comforting me—just like when I was a child. Her soothing words were a balm to my soul. No longer did I feel the pain in my foot; and the great heaviness in my heart felt a little lighter. I longed for her to stay. Her loving presence was to me like water to a man dying of thirst. I drank it up and felt I could go on drinking forever.

"'Nathaniel,' she said. 'I gave my life to bring love back into the world. It is here for you! Let go of anger. Let go of hate. Embrace love!'

"When my mother's presence left I felt an overwhelming sense of loss. It was as raw and as new as the day she had died. There was a great gaping hole inside of me—a vacuum that cried out to be filled. I had learned in the past to fill that hole with hate. I knew now that I needed to fill it with love.

"It has been a painful journey to bring love back into my life. But every time I begin to slip back into the habit of hate, I remember my mother's words—'Embrace love!'

Embracing love has shown me a new view of the world. I have learned about the balance of the yin and the yang and how essential that balance is. It was hard for me to accept this at first. I was skeptical of letting yin values gain any ground. I thought that allowing yin to emerge would just mean more dominance and control—but this time the control would be disguised as love.

"Gradually I began to gain a new understanding. Yin values don't seek dominance: it is *unnatural* to them. I realized it is not dangerous to let love reign supreme. Love will never—can never—become a cruel dictator. Love is described by the ancient scripture as patient, kind, and incapable of evil. Love is not selfish or vain and it endures. I realized there was no reason for me to fear love, and that embracing it as my highest value was the only way to eliminate fear in my life. With love as the highest value in the kingdom, leadership won't need to seek power and dominance. Love will flow out from the leadership to serve people and love will flow back from the people to the leader— an ebb and flow of perfect balance.

"Today, Coronation Day, I have a special proclamation to make for this kingdom. I hereby proclaim that all men are kings and all women are queens! We do not need the monarchy to say one person is more valuable than the next. You are valued as highly as kings and queens! And you are bound by only one duty: the duty to hold love as your highest value."

The crowd gasped. "What does this mean?"

Nathaniel recognized their shock and uncertainty about his new idea. "I know this sounds radical and frightening to you. Do not despair. I am not suggesting anarchy. I will remain as a leader for you—but leading from my heart not from a throne! Together we can learn to embrace love and discover a new era of love and peace on Earth. What an exciting adventure we have ahead of us! Are you ready for it?"

Nathaniel looked out across the crowd into the faces of the people. He saw expressions of bewilderment as they considered his words. Then a voice called out from the farthest corner of the crowd. "Yes!" A woman stood, holding a child in her arms. "Yes! I am ready!" A man stood next and said, "Yes!" More men and women stood and joined in. Soon the crowd was on its feet saying, "Yes! Yes! Yes!"

Nathaniel spoke into the loudspeaker, "Welcome, Kings and Queens! I have a coronation gift for you today. Here in the center of the garden is a mosaic. The tiles have been fashioned out of the metal from the weapons left here in the garden. This mosaic is here to remind us of the beauty of peace, and the terrible consequence of war. It reminds us to keep the yin and yang in balance to maintain peace forevermore.

Nathaniel signalled to the palace personnel to remove the tent that had been covering the mosaic. As the tent was pulled aside, the people beheld a beautiful work of art. The yin and yang symbol showed perfect balance in its stark black and white. A rose adorned the symbol, signifying love and peace. The tiles had an iridescent quality to them, reflecting the faces of the people who looked upon them. As the crowd circled around the mosaic, Nathaniel approached a cornerstone with an inscription carved into it. He said, "I will leave you today by reading the words of the inscription. It is from the prophet Isaiah:

And they shall beat their swords into plowshares, and their spears into pruninghooks: nation shall not lift up sword against nation, neither shall they learn war any more.

Isaiah 2:4

After Nathaniel read the words, the crowd stood silently. Some wiped tears from their eyes. Others hugged one another. No one seemed to want to disturb the sacredness of the moment.

Sarah had remained seated throughout the program, contemplating the words the King said and the magnitude of his proclamation. She looked at the mosaic of the yin and the yang in the center of the courtyard. Pressing her hands together in front of her, with her thumbs touching her breastbone, she said softly, "The vision is complete. I am free to go now." She lowered her head as if in prayer.

After a few moments she raised her head and started shifting her weight in preparation to stand. The crowd was beginning to disperse. Two women approached her from across the garden. They looked deeply into Sarah's eyes and said, "We are here to help you."

Sarah noted their beauty, especially their eyes. One woman's were as clear and as blue as a sun-stained piece of glass. The other's were as black as pure obsidian. The presence of the two mystery women made Sarah feel safe and comfortable. "Yes," she said. "I welcome your help." Sarah lifted up her right hand to one woman and her left hand to the other so they could support her on both sides. They lifted Sarah up and helped her gain her balance. The three walked slowly to the edge of the garden. They followed the lazy stream for a while and disappeared together into the distance.

Diane Wolverton is the State Director of the Wyoming Small Business Development Center. She is a frequent speaker at women's groups and has led numerous workshops and retreats. She holds a Master's Degree from the University of Wyoming and is currently working on her doctoral degree at the University of Creation Spirituality in Oakland, California.